TIGER in My SOUP

For my brother Amit
—K. S.

To my best friend Jim
—J. E.

Ω

Published by
PEACHTREE PUBLISHERS
1700 Chattahoochee Avenue
Atlanta, Georgia 30318-2112
www.peachtree-online.com

Book design by Jeffrey Ebbeler
Cover design by Loraine M. Joyner

Illustrations created in acrylic on archival 100% rag watercolor
paper. Text typeset in Microsoft's Tw Cen MT; title typeset in
Island of Misfit Toys by Steve Ferrera.

Printed in February 2015 in the United States of America
by Worzalla in Stevens Point, WI

10 9 8 7 6 5 4 3 (hardcover)
10 9 8 7 6 5 4 3 2 1 (trade paperback)

Library of Congress Cataloging-in-Publication Data

Sheth, Kashmira.
  Tiger in my soup / written by Kashmira Sheth ; illustrated by
Jeffrey Ebbeler.
      p. cm.
  Summary: Left in the care of his older sister, a boy begs her
to read his favorite book but she is too absorbed in her own
reading even to notice when a tiger comes to life in the steam
from his soup.
    ISBN 978-1-56145-696-3 (hardcover)
    ISBN 978-1-56145-890-5 (trade paperback)
[1. Books and reading—Fiction. 2. Brothers and sisters—Fiction.
3. Babysitters—Fiction.] I. Ebbeler, Jeffrey, ill. II. Title.
PZ7.S5543Tig 2013
[E]—dc23
                                                    2012025539

TIGER IN MY SOUP

Kashmira Sheth

Illustrated by
Jeffrey Ebbeler

PEACHTREE
ATLANTA

Today, my big sister
is in charge of
the house, the
lunch, and
me.

I hold up my book.

"Will you read to me?" I ask.

"Not now," she says.

I look at the pictures by myself...

downside up and upside down,

with my eyes open and
with my eyes closed.

front to back and back to front,

But it's no fun

doing it by myself.

"Will you read my book to me?" I ask again. "It's about tigers.

Big, hungry tigers."

My sister doesn't answer.
I try something else.

My sister gives me a bowl of soup for lunch. "Be careful," she says. "It's hot."

"While the soup cools, will you read to me?" I beg.

"Later," she says.

I stir my soup. Something steamy puffs up.

A tiger! There's a tiger in my soup!

I drop my spoon. I glance over at my sister.

"Help!"

"*Grrrrr,*" my sister grumbles.
She hands me a clean spoon.

The tiger looks really mad.

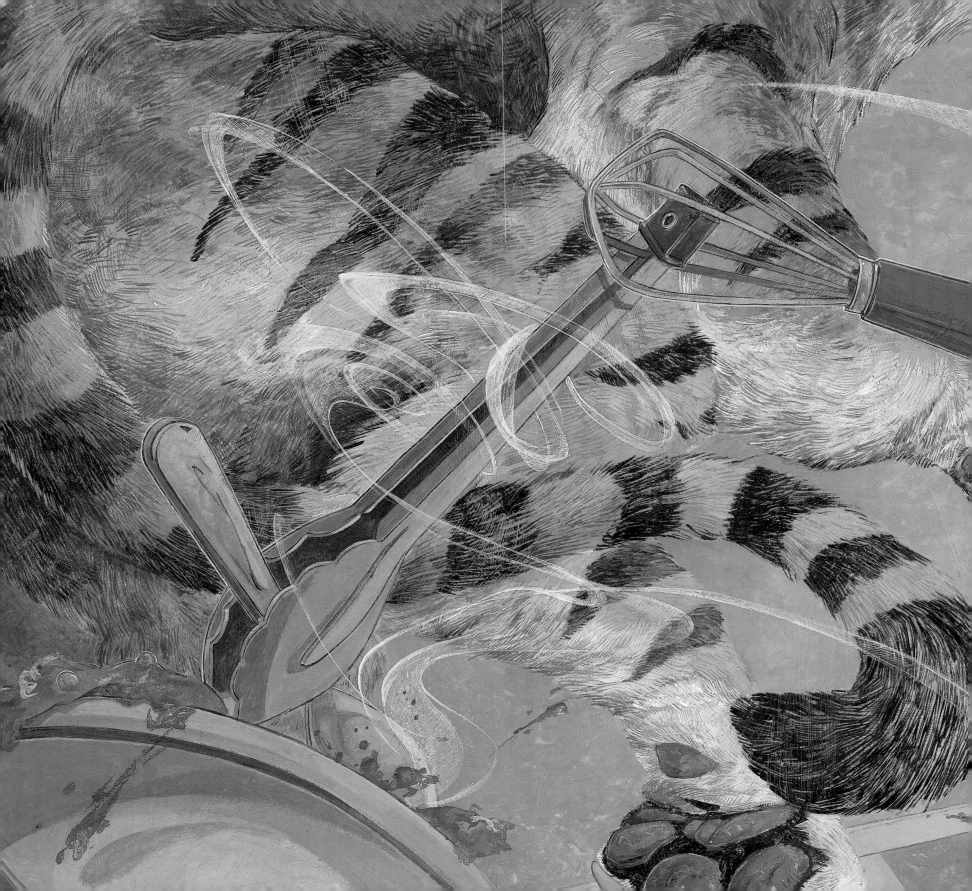

I have to protect myself. I stab at him with my spoon. Some tiger spit lands on my face.

I launch a missile
at the tiger.

Right on target!

My sister looks up from her book. "Why'd you let your soup get cold?" she asks. "Here, I'll warm it up."

"Look out for the tiger!"

It's too late.

The tiger's muffled roar rumbles from inside the microwave.

"Hide!"
I yell.
"It's a big,
hungry tiger!"

"Okay," my sister sighs.

"Where's your book?"

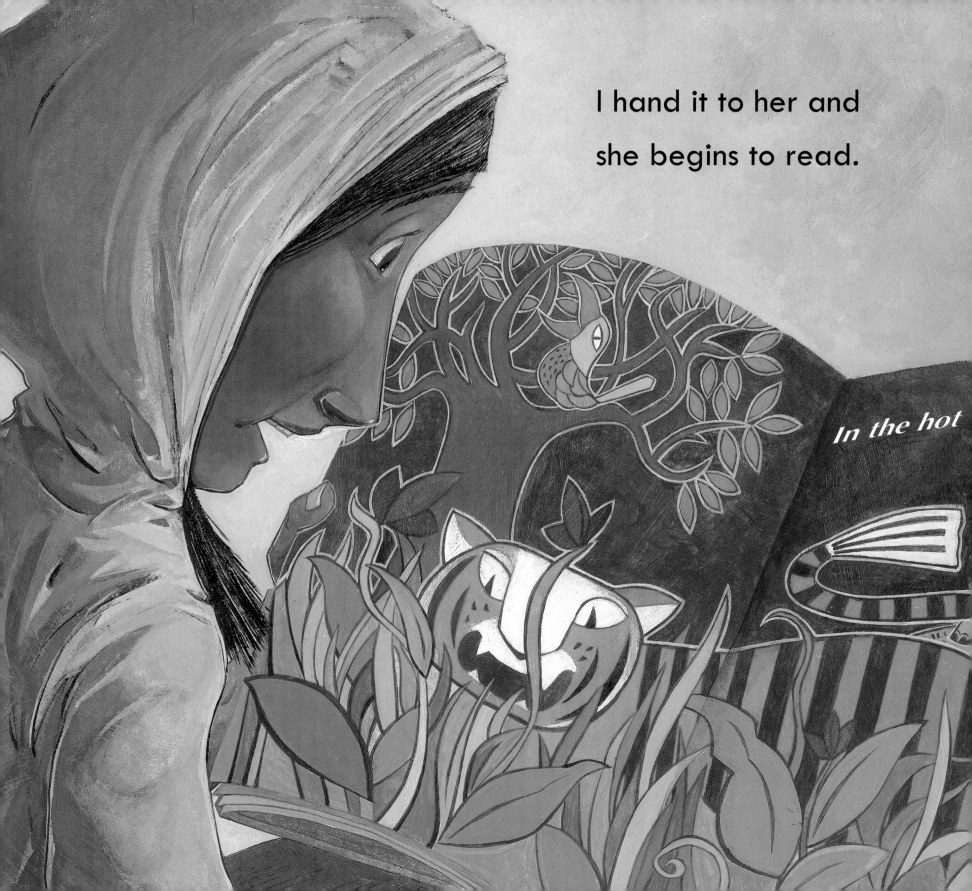

I hand it to her and
she begins to read.

In the hot

"No, no," I say.
"You have to roar
like a tiger."

steamy jungle there was a loud roar...

I eat my soup and keep one eye on my sister.
I wonder where the tiger will show up next.